Battle Buddies

Senior Art Editor Anna Formanek
Project Editor Lara Hutcheson
Production Editor Marc Staples
Senior Production Controller Lloyd Robertson
Managing Editor Tori Kosara
Managing Art Editor Jo Connor
Publisher Paula Regan
Managing Director Mark Searle

Written by Lara Hutcheson
Designed for DK by Thelma-Jane Robb
Reading Consultant Barbara Marinak

DK would like to thank Hank Woon, Alyssa Tuffey, and the rest of the team at The Pokémon Company International. Thanks also to Julia March for proofreading, and Emma Wicks for design assistance.

First American Edition, 2025
Published in the United States by DK Publishing Publishing,
a division of Penguin Random House LLC
1745 Broadway, 20th Floor, New York, NY 10019

© 2025 Pokémon. © 1997–2023 Nintendo, Creatures, GAME FREAK,
TV Tokyo, ShoPro, JR Kikaku. TM, ® Nintendo
25 26 27 28 29 10 9 8 7 6 5 4 3 2 1
001–344851–Feb/2025

All rights reserved.
Without limiting the rights under the copyright reserved above, no part of this publication may be reproduced, stored in or introduced into a retrieval system, or transmitted, in any form, or by any means (electronic, mechanical, photocopying, recording, or otherwise), without the prior written permission of the copyright owner.
Published in Great Britain by Dorling Kindersley Limited

A catalog record for this book is available from the Library of Congress.
ISBN 978-0-5939-5999-2 (Paperback)
ISBN 978-0-5939-6000-4 (Hardcover)

DK books are available at special discounts when purchased
in bulk for sales promotions, premiums, fund-raising, or educational use.
For details, contact: DK Publishing Special Markets,
1745 Broadway, 20th Floor, New York, NY 10019
SpecialSales@dk.com

Printed and bound in Canada

www.dk.com

This book was made with Forest Stewardship Council™ certified paper—one small step in DK's commitment to a sustainable future.
Learn more at www.dk.com/uk/information/sustainability

Level 2

Battle Buddies

DK

Contents

- 6   Pokémon battles
- 8   Pokémon Trainers
- 10   A special bond
- 12   Pokémon schools
- 14   Amazing battle moves
- 16   Helpful moves
- 18   Friede and Charizard
- 20   Captain Pikachu
- 22   Ceruledge
- 24   Small and mighty
- 26   Time to heal
- 28   Nidothing
- 30   Glossary
- 31   Index
- 32   Quiz

Pokémon battles

Pokémon love to battle against each other. To try and beat their opponents, they can use lots of exciting special moves.

Captain's hat

Captain Pikachu

Captain Pikachu enjoys the challenge of a battle.

Tail shaped like a lightning bolt

Battle ready

Captain Pikachu can use powerful Electric-type moves.

Pokémon Trainers

A Pokémon Trainer catches Pokémon and coaches them in battle. A Trainer needs to be good friends with their Pokémon to get the very best out of them.

Fuecoco

Roy is a Pokémon Trainer.
He has a great friendship with his partner Pokémon, Fuecoco.

A special bond

When a Trainer and their Pokémon know each other well, they become a stronger force in battle.

Liko watches Sprigatito very closely. She wants to learn more about her Pokémon.

Liko

Sprigatito

Liko sometimes finds it hard to know what Sprigatito is thinking!

Pokémon schools

A Pokémon school is a place where Trainers learn all about Pokémon and battling. Students bring their Pokémon friends along to the lessons.

Indigo Academy

This is a school in the Kanto region. It has an area where students can practice battling.

Amazing battle moves

There are lots of different moves that a Pokémon can use to try and win a battle. A great Trainer knows which moves will work best against certain Pokémon.

Roy's Wattrel uses Spark.

Rhydon uses Rock Blast.

Spark attack

Roy's Wattrel can use an awesome Electric-type move called Spark.
To make the battle move stronger, Roy and Wattrel spend time practicing.

Helpful moves

Sometimes a Pokémon might use a special move when they are not in battle.

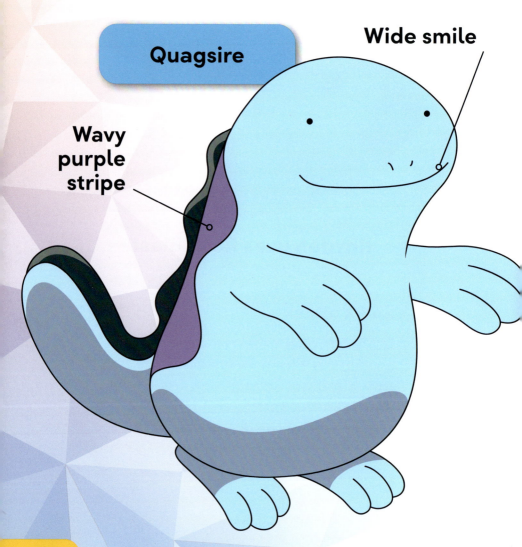

Quagsire's Rain Dance move.

Quagsire has a move called Rain Dance. The move makes it rain and helps forests to grow.

17

Friede and Charizard

Friede is a Pokémon Professor. He often chooses to use his Charizard in battle.

Charizard is fierce and strong.

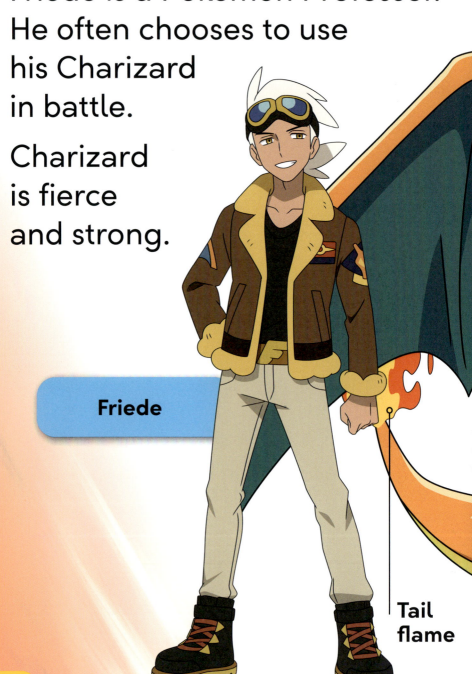

Friede

Tail flame

Captain Pikachu

Captain Pikachu is in Friede's Pokémon team.

It has lots of exciting and powerful moves it can use in battle.

Double Team

Double Team is a move that can confuse opponents. Lots of Pikachu will appear, but only one is the real Pikachu!

Thunder Punch

Captain Pikachu uses its mighty Thunder Punch.

Volt Tackle

A Volt Tackle move can cause lots of damage.

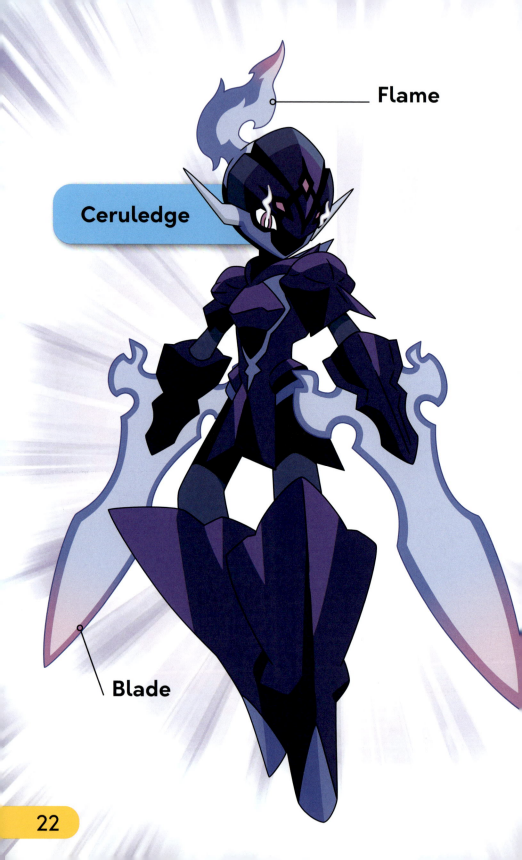

Ceruledge

Ceruledge is a very scary Pokémon to face in battle. It fights using the blades on its arms.

Watch out for its sharp Bitter Blade move!

Small and mighty

Pokémon come in all shapes and sizes, but size doesn't always matter in battle.

Sprigatito's Scratch

Liko's Sprigatito is small, but by using its Scratch move it can put up a big fight!

Powerful Pawmo

Pawmo wins a battle against the larger Skiploom.

A smaller Pokémon can sometimes win against a bigger one.

Its moves might be more powerful, or it might have more energy.

Time to heal

After a tricky battle, Pokémon need time to recover.

They might be tired, or even injured.

Mollie

Chansey

Mollie and Chansey help Pokémon who are unwell. They can make them feel much better.

Pink tufts

Egg in pouch

Nidothing

Nidothing is a popular video streamer.

Nidothing

Large zip on costume

She wears a cool costume and makes videos packed with helpful tips for Pokémon Trainers.

Nidothing's battle tips
- Get to know your Pokémon
- Keep practicing
- Have fun!

Glossary

Challenge
A difficult task or problem.

Costume
Clothing worn to make someone look like another person or thing.

Opponent
Someone that is competing against another.

Poké Ball
A ball used by Trainers to catch and carry Pokémon.

Pokémon move
Action that a Pokémon uses for attack or defense.

Pokémon Professor
An expert in Pokémon.

Pokémon Trainer
Someone who raises Pokémon and battles with them in competition.

Popular
Liked or enjoyed by many people.

Video streamer
Someone who creates videos to share online.

Index

B
Bitter Blade 23

C
Captain Pikachu 6–7, 20–21
Ceruledge 22–23
Chansey 26–27
Charizard 18–19

D
Double Team 20

E
Electric-type moves 7, 15

F
Friede 18, 20
Fuecoco 9

I
Indigo Academy 12–13

L
Liko 10–11

M
Mollie 26–27

N
Nidothing 28–29

P
Pawmo 25
Poké Ball 8
Pokémon Schools 12–13
Pokémon Trainers 9, 10–11, 12, 14, 29

Q
Quagsire 16–17

R
Rain Dance 17
Rhydon 15
Rock Blast 15
Roy 8–9, 15

S
Scratch 24
Skiploom 25
Spark 14–15
Sprigatito 10–11, 24
Thunder Punch 21

V
Volt Tackle 21

W
Wattrel 14–15

Quiz

It's time to find out how much you have learned! Read the questions and then check the answers with an adult.

1. Who is Roy's partner Pokémon?
2. Can Captain Pikachu do a move called Double Team?
3. What did Quagsire's Rain Dance move do?
4. Does Ceruledge have blades on its arms?
5. What is inside Chansey's pouch?

1. Fuecoco 2. Yes 3. Make it rain 4. Yes 5. An egg